LOCKER 37

The Magic Eraser

by Aaron Starmer
illustrated by Courtney La Forest

Penguin Workshop

To Rowan—AS

For my dearest sister, Erika, the Carson to
my Riley—thank you for always supporting
and loving so wholly anyone lucky enough to
know you. You inspire me to not fear making
mistakes—even without a magical eraser—CLF

W

PENGUIN WORKSHOP
An Imprint of Penguin Random House LLC, New York

Penguin supports copyright. Copyright fuels creativity, encourages diverse voices, promotes free speech, and creates a vibrant culture. Thank you for buying an authorized edition of this book and for complying with copyright laws by not reproducing, scanning, or distributing any part of it in any form without permission. You are supporting writers and allowing Penguin to continue to publish books for every reader.

The publisher does not have any control over and does not assume any responsibility for author or third-party websites or their content.

Photo credits: pages 36–39 (lock vector) Peterpal/iStock/Getty Images Plus, (line icons) justinroque/iStock/Getty Images Plus

Text copyright © 2020 by Aaron Starmer. Illustrations copyright © 2020 by Penguin Random House LLC. All rights reserved. Published by Penguin Workshop, an imprint of Penguin Random House LLC, New York. PENGUIN and PENGUIN WORKSHOP are trademarks of Penguin Books Ltd, and the W colophon is a registered trademark of Penguin Random House LLC. Manufactured in China.

Visit us online at www.penguinrandomhouse.com.

Library of Congress Cataloging-in-Publication Data is available upon request.

ISBN 9780593222850 (pbk)   10 9 8 7 6 5 4 3 2 1
ISBN 9780593094280 (hc)   10 9 8 7 6 5 4 3 2 1

Chapter One

HOPEWELL ELEMENTARY

Before the first day of fourth grade, Carson Cooper thought Hopewell Elementary was exactly like any other school. It had classrooms for math, art, and science. It had a cafetorium, which was a cafeteria during the day and an auditorium at night. It had a gym with a climbing rope and something called a pommel horse in it.

(A pommel horse is exactly like a regular horse—that is, if the regular horse only has two legs and doesn't have hair, or a neck, or a head, but instead has handles on its back and stands entirely still so that gymnasts can jump on it.)

In the front of Hopewell Elementary, near the stone steps leading up to the entrance, there was a big NO SKATEBOARDING! sign that was often ignored. Behind the school, there was a dumpster, full of things best left unseen and unsmelled.

From September through June, Hopewell Elementary was full of students and teachers, who were mostly nice, most of the time. Carson didn't love going there, but he'd been going there since kindergarten, so he was used to it. And he was used to thinking it was an entirely normal place.

It was *not* an entirely normal place.

In fact, Hopewell Elementary was the strangest, most amazing place in the universe. And that's saying a lot. The universe had pulsars, black holes, and indoor water parks in it.

Those places were nothing compared to Hopewell Elementary. Hopewell Elementary had Locker 37 in it.

Locker 37 made all the difference.

Chapter Two
LOCKER 37

Locker 37 was at the east end of the
school, past the music room, in a
dimly lit corner near a janitor closet full
of toilet paper and laundry detergent.
It was four feet tall, metal, and green. It
had three slits in the door that worked as
vents. It had a spinning combination lock
with the numbers zero through forty-
nine on it.

On the outside, it looked like all the other lockers. So there was never any reason to suspect it was different on the inside.

But, boy, was it different on the inside.

Every day it was different.

Anyone who knew the combination knew that.

And on the first day of every school year, one lucky fourth-grader (or unlucky fourth-grader, depending on how you look at it) would learn the combination.

Chapter Three

MRS. SHEN

"**W**elcome, friends, to the best year of your life," Mrs. Shen said to Carson Cooper's homeroom on the first day of fourth grade.

It didn't seem like an exaggeration. According to just about everyone, Mrs. Shen was the school's best teacher. She told jokes that were actually funny. She held trivia contests. She showed

YouTube videos in class. Having her as homeroom teacher guaranteed a good year. Being a fourth-grader made things even better.

Fourth-graders were the kings and queens of Hopewell Elementary. They were the oldest and wisest. They knew the school's secrets. For instance:

- Always buy school lunch on taco day, but never, ever, ever on fish stick day.
- The bathroom in the basement of the school is known as the Dungeon. Why? Because it looks like a dungeon, smells like a dungeon, and going to

the bathroom in it is like a form of medieval torture. Avoid the Dungeon at all costs.

- Locker 37 can do anything. And by anything, that means ANYTHING.

Carson learned this last secret right after Mrs. Shen told him this would be the best year of his life. That was when his knee brushed against something. Reaching down, he found a folded piece of paper stuck with a wad of chewing gum to the bottom of his desk.

He peeled the paper off. He sniffed the gum.

Watermelon.

Then he unfolded the paper.

It was a note.

Chapter Four

THE NOTE

Dear Fourth-Grader,
   Congratulations on finding this incredibly important note!
   You are now the keeper of the combination to locker 37. locker 37 has helped fourth-graders at Hopewell Elementary for decades. We know it will help you, too.
   If you or another fourth-grader has a problem (any problem!),

open locker 37 and the locker will provide a solution. It won't always be the solution you want, or expect, but it is guaranteed to work.

Only fourth-graders

know about locker 37. So feel free to tell all your friends in fourth grade about it. It's encouraged!

But don't tell anyone younger. And don't ask anyone older for advice. Everyone who finishes fourth grade immediately forgets about locker 37. You will, too.

In the meantime, have fun. And best of luck!

Sincerely,
Last year's fourth-graders

P.S. We almost forgot to give you the combination! It's 43-12-29.

P.P.S. Oh yeah, and locker 37 can do anything. And by anything, we mean ANYTHING! No big deal.

P.P.P.S. Your life is about to get bonkers. Extremely bonkers.

P.P.P.P.S. Feel free to chew the gum.

Chapter Five

THE STAIN

Carson had a problem.

Actually, he had a few problems.

- He had forgotten to bring his lunch, so he would have to buy lunch. And it was fish stick day.
- He didn't understand how to multiply fractions. He had passed third grade, which meant

he was supposed to understand how to multiply fractions. But he still didn't understand how to multiply fractions.

- He was sort of tempted to chew that watermelon gum. Yes, he knew it was gross, but watermelon was his absolute favorite flavor.

Forget those problems, though. Because he had one problem that was bigger than all the others combined.

Carson had a stain on his pants.

It might not sound like much to worry about, until you realize where the stain was. It was in a place on Carson's pants where nobody ever wants to see a stain. Ever.

No, not his thigh, or his shin, or the back of his knee. You know exactly where it was.

Now do you get it?

Carson noticed the stain as soon as he slipped the mysterious note about Locker 37 into his pants pocket. The stain wasn't there when he got dressed in the morning, so he wondered how it could have found its way onto his pants.

Did he sit on something wet while riding the bus?

Did he bump into something gross in the hall?

Did he rub against something nasty on the bottom of his desk? Watermelon gum, for instance?

Ultimately, it didn't matter where the stain came from. All that mattered was that it was there. It was big, and dark, and splotchy. It made Carson want to scream out loud.

Mrs. Shen was still talking, so Carson held the scream in.

"I'd like to introduce our class mascots. Meet Finn and Gill," she said as she pointed to a pair of goldfish swimming in a bowl on a table in the back next to the radiator. "Would anyone in class be interested in feeding them every day?"

A hand shot up and a voice called out, "I think I've shown how responsible I can be, as a founding member and president of the Junior Janitor Club. So I should be in charge of the fishies."

"Fair enough," Mrs. Shen said. "And what's your name?"

"Keisha James, ma'am."

"Thank you, and nice to make your acquaintance, Keisha. Is anyone else interested in feeding the fishes?"

The question was met with silence. The other students already knew Keisha was the best person for the job. She was an overachiever of the highest order, and had been nominating herself for positions since kindergarten.

"It's settled, then," Mrs. Shen said. "Keisha will feed Finn and Gill. And I've also learned a little bit about her. So what about the rest of the class? I realize that many of you already know one another. But I don't know most of you. When I call out your name, tell me something interesting about yourself."

What was interesting about Carson? He didn't have the faintest idea. All he could think about was the embarrassment on his pants, and all he could do was stare at it. The stain was both terrifying and hypnotizing, and so he hardly heard Mrs. Shen when she called out, "Sarah Abramson."

And he hardly heard Sarah when she responded, "Hi. I'm Sarah, and I like to juggle."

He certainly didn't see Sarah pull a pencil, a glue stick, and a ruler out of her backpack and start juggling them while still sitting at her desk. Which was too bad, because she was circus-level good.

Mrs. Shen cheered and clapped. So did most of the class.

Except for Carson. His hands and eyes remained on his lap. So when Mrs. Shen called out other names, in alphabetical order, he also missed that . . .

Kendall Ali liked to cook . . .

Hayley Baker could say the alphabet backward . . .

And Nina Camacho knew more about lemurs than most lemurologists (which is the technical term for a lemur scientist, right?).

Inevitably, it was Carson's turn. When Mrs. Shen called out his name, Carson was still distracted. That's why he answered with one word.

"Pants," Carson said.

"Pants?" Mrs. Shen replied. "Do you mean you . . . *like* pants?"

Carson was too embarrassed to say anything else, so he nodded.

"I like pants, too," Mrs. Shen said with a warm smile. "One of the world's best inventions for hiding your underwear."

The class laughed. Carson lowered his head. And Mrs. Shen saved him from more embarrassment by calling on other students.

Luckily, no one in class seemed to notice the stain. Carson knew that it was only a matter of time, though. Getting rid of the stain became his number one priority.

He pulled the note out of his pocket and read the most important part of it again.

If you or another fourth-grader has a problem (any problem!), open locker 37 and the locker will provide a solution.

Chapter Six

HUNTER BARNES

Carson hurried from homeroom toward Locker 37. He had a sweatshirt tied around his waist to hide the stain, but somehow Hunter Barnes still saw it.

Hunter pointed and said, "Check it out. Carson had an accident."

It was true that the kids and teachers at Hopewell Elementary were mostly nice, most of the time. Hunter Barnes was the exception.

Hunter wasn't a bully in the traditional sense. He didn't punch, kick, or even push anyone. He didn't threaten people, either. By every measurement, he was one of the smallest kids in fourth grade.

Still, he was a bully.

His favorite thing to do was humiliate his classmates. He had a natural ability to see things that others were trying to hide. And he would

reveal those hidden things to everyone.

To EVERYONE!

"Where are you going, Carson?" Hunter yelled. "To the bathroom? Didn't you already relieve yourself? All over your stained PANTS?"

Then Hunter cackled.

Carson put his head down and kept moving.

He passed the art room, but he could still hear laughter behind him . . .

He passed the gym and the laughter was fainter . . .

He hurried, faster and faster . . .

He held the sweatshirt tight to make sure it didn't fall off . . .

He pushed his way through crowds . . .

He jogged past the music room and the

sounds of cymbals crashing . . .

He kept going . . .

Until it was quiet . . .

And he was alone . . .

In the dark hallway that led to Locker 37.

Chapter Seven

WHAT IF?

People leave clothes in lockers all the time. So Carson thought it was possible that Locker 37 might have a clean pair of pants in it. That were his style . . . and his size.

Possible, though not likely.

It seemed more likely that the note was a joke and that the locker was empty. At the very least, Carson thought he would have a moment by himself to figure out what to do.

Carson knew this hallway well, and knew it was one of the darkest and loneliest parts of school. Only third- and fourth-graders went down the hallway, because they were the only ones who used lockers. The other kids used classroom cubbies.

In third grade, Carson's locker was Locker 28, and he remembered sometimes seeing groups of fourth-graders hanging around Locker 37. Sometimes they were laughing. Sometimes they were gasping. They were *always* whispering. He figured it was because they were up to some sort of mischief. Fourth-grade mischief, in particular, which was the most mischievous variety.

Now that he was a fourth-grader with the combination to Locker 37, Carson was about to discover that this wasn't about mischief. Or, to be more accurate, this was only *partly* about mischief.

He placed his hand on the dial of the lock.

He looked over his shoulder to make sure he was still alone.

He was.

He began to turn the dial.

43.

12.

29.

And . . .

Wait a second.

Before we get to the part where

Carson opens the locker, let's consider a question: How lucky was Carson to know about Locker 37 and its combination?

Answer: very lucky.

Because what if he didn't know about Locker 37 and its combination? What if the only thing Carson knew was that there was a locker somewhere in school that solved problems? How easy would it be for him to find this problem-solving locker and open it?

Answer: not very easy.

Want proof? Keep reading.

Chapter Eight

THE "WAIT A SECOND, IS THIS A MATH CHAPTER?" CHAPTER

How long would it take Carson to open Locker 37 if he didn't have that helpful note from last year's fourth-graders? Let's do the arithmetic and see!

(Feel free to pull out a pencil and paper and follow along. Or feel free to skip this chapter. The author and your math teacher will be very disappointed, but hey, it's your life.)

**ONE 3-NUMBER
COMBINATION
=
10 SECONDS
TO DIAL**

It takes about 10 seconds to dial a 3-number combination. Try it. Get a padlock. Time yourself. If you can dial a combination faster, pat yourself on the back and take the rest of the day off. Because you're exceptional. But for most people, it will take about 10 seconds.

Let's assume Carson was like most people.

**1 MINUTE
=
60 SECONDS
60 SECONDS
÷
10 SECONDS
=
6 COMBINATIONS
PER MINUTE**

There are 60 seconds in 1 minute, which means Carson could realistically try 6 combinations in 1 minute. That number 6 comes from taking 60 seconds and dividing them by 10 seconds per combination.

There are 60 minutes in 1 hour, so that's 360 combinations in 1 hour, or 6 combinations per minute multiplied by 60 minutes.

6 COMBINATIONS PER MINUTE

×

60 MINUTES

=

360 COMBINATIONS PER HOUR

1 HOUR
=
60 MINUTES

The Hopewell Elementary school day runs from 7:30 a.m. to 2:30 p.m. That's 7 hours in 1 school day.

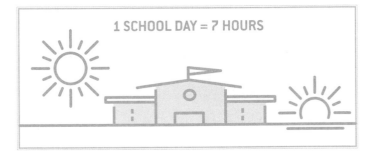

1 SCHOOL DAY = 7 HOURS

360 COMBINATIONS PER HOUR

×

7 HOURS

=

2,520 COMBINATIONS PER SCHOOL DAY

Dialing 360 combinations per hour for 7 hours (or 360 multiplied by 7) means that on an average school day at Hopewell Elementary, Carson could try 2,520 combinations.

Pretty good, right?

ZZZ

Pretty tiring, actually.

Because Carson couldn't stop to eat lunch, chat with friends, or even take a bathroom break! All he could do for the entire school day is turn that dial. And it gets worse!

The dial had 50 numbers on it (0 to 49).

50 NUMBERS ON
THE DIAL

To figure out the number of possible 3-number combinations, multiply 50 by 50 by 50. Mathematicians call this 50 to the third power.

50 NUMBERS ON
THE DIAL
×
3 NUMBERS IN
THE COMBINATION

It sounds *powerful.*

$50 \times 50 \times 50$
=
50^3

It is powerful! The result is 125,000 possible combinations!

$$50^3 = 125,000$$

To try all 125,000 possible combinations, it would take Carson nearly 50 full school days. That's 125,000 combinations divided by 2,520 combinations per school day. (Which actually equals 49.6031746032, but why don't we round up to 50 because we don't hate ourselves, okay?)

125,000 COMBINATIONS

÷

2,520 COMBINATIONS PER SCHOOL DAY

=

50 SCHOOL DAYS TO TRY EVERY COMBINATION

Since there are 5 school days in a week, we can take 50 school days divided by 5 days per week to learn that it would take 10 full school weeks of doing nothing but turning a dial.

50 SCHOOL DAYS

÷

5 DAYS PER WEEK

=

10 SCHOOL WEEKS

Looks like Carson is going to fail fourth grade!

But wait, it gets worse.

This is assuming Carson knew which locker to try. What if he didn't?

There were 400 lockers in Hopewell Elementary. Many of those lockers were unused, but Carson didn't know which ones were full of books, which ones were empty, and which ones were magical.

Assuming Carson tried the lockers in numerical order, starting with Locker 1, he would reach Locker 37 relatively early in the process. This would take 370 weeks of school, or 10 weeks of school per locker multiplied by 37 lockers.

> 10 SCHOOL WEEKS PER LOCKER TO TRY ALL COMBINATIONS
>
> ×
>
> 37 LOCKERS
>
> =
>
> 370 WEEKS

There are 40 weeks in the school year at Hopewell Elementary. So, 370 weeks of trying lockers divided by 40 weeks per year equals 9 ¼ years.

370 WEEKS
÷
40 WEEKS IN THE SCHOOL YEAR
=
9 ¼ YEARS

Again, that's 9 ¼ years.

YEARS!

9 ¼ YEARS!!!

What that means is this: When most of Carson's classmates would be starting college, Carson would have failed fourth grade 9 times. But he also would have finally opened that problem-solving locker. Hooray!

But what if he tried the lockers in random order? And what if, by random chance, the last locker he tried was Locker 37?

400 lockers times 10 weeks per locker divided by 40 weeks per school year means Carson would be spinning combination dials for 7 hours a day, 5 days a week, 40 weeks a year, for . . . 100 YEARS.

Congratulations, Carson! You are now 109 years old, officially the oldest fourth-grader in the world. Enjoy the locker that solves problems! Your biggest problem is that you're now probably dead.

400 LOCKERS
×
10 WEEKS PER LOCKER
÷
40 WEEKS PER SCHOOL YEAR
=
100 YEARS

This is all a very complicated (and very educational!) way to say that Carson was lucky. It would be basically impossible for someone to find and open Locker 37 without first discovering that note.

This is a good thing. Because guess what was inside Locker 37?

Chapter Nine

THE THING THAT WAS INSIDE LOCKER 37

An eraser.

A pink eraser.

A pink rubber eraser that fit in the palm of a hand.

That was all that Carson found in Locker 37. He held it, and stared at it, until someone said something.

"Hunter Barnes is a real slime."

It was Riley Zimmerman, Carson's

best friend. Carson turned to find her

lingering in the hall a few yards away.

Closing his hand over the eraser and

looking down at the stain, Carson said,

"Yeah, Hunter is the worst."

Riley stepped forward and gave Carson a playful punch on the arm. "You can wear my gym shorts if you want."

"Thanks, but I don't know if that's the solution," Carson said, because he knew that wearing Riley's neon green gym shorts would attract even more attention. And Hunter would tease him even more, especially since they were a girl's shorts.

"What're you doing down here, anyway?" Riley asked.

Carson shrugged. "A note told me that Locker 37 could solve my problem."

(Remember: The note also told him that he could tell other fourth-graders about Locker 37, so Carson saw no harm in mentioning it to his closest friend.)

"Don't believe everything you read," Riley said as she peered over Carson's shoulder to Locker 37. "So what'd ya find in there?"

"This," Carson said, and he held the eraser up.

Snatching the eraser and looking at it closely, Riley said, "Well, it *is* an eraser."

"It looks like it's for pencils, though," Carson said with a sigh. "My problem is bigger than pencil marks."

There was writing on the eraser that Carson hadn't noticed. But Riley's keen eye caught it. "It says *Rub Three Times*," she told Carson.

"I wish things were that simple," Carson said.

Maybe they were.

Because out of curiosity, Riley walked to the other side of the hall, where there weren't any lockers. She held the eraser out and rubbed it on a brick in the wall.

One time.

Two times.

Three times.

Suddenly sunlight poured into the dark hallway. There was now a hole in the wall. The brick had disappeared.

Chapter Ten
DISAPPEARANCES

"Holy ravioli!" Riley cried as she stuck her hand through the hole and felt the warm September air. "It's gone!"

It sure was. The hole in the wall was the exact same size and shape as the brick. There was no rubble on the ground. There was no dust. It was like popping a bubble. The brick was there, and then—*pop!*

Terrified, Riley dropped the eraser.

Terrified again, she jumped back and yelled, "Watch out! The floor might disappear!"

The floor didn't disappear. Because the eraser was smarter than that.

"It says *Rub Three Times* on it," Carson told her as he picked it up. "Maybe that's so it doesn't make things disappear by accident."

Carson put it to the test. He paced over to a locked janitor closet at the end of the hall. He rubbed the eraser on the doorknob once.

Nothing.

Two times.

Nope.

Three times. *Pop.* Just like that, the doorknob was gone.

"Holy rigatoni!" Riley cried, and the door swung open to reveal a shelf of laundry detergent and five more shelves stacked with rolls of the world's driest, scratchiest, cheapest toilet paper.

"We've gotta get outta here," Carson said.

"No, we've gotta cover our tracks first," Riley said.

Thinking quickly, Riley peeled a poster off the wall. The poster said MISTAKES ARE PROOF THAT YOU'RE TRYING. She placed it over the hole where the brick once was.

Then she wadded up some toilet paper and jammed the wad under the door of the janitor closet. It did the trick. It kept it closed.

"Now can we go?" Carson asked.

Riley's answer was to run away, as fast as she could. Carson slipped the eraser in his pocket and followed.

Chapter Eleven

THE LEGS DILEMMA

Carson was too scared to use the eraser. It stayed in his pocket through the morning. But of course it was the only thing he could think about.

By the time lunch came around, he decided to take it out of his pocket. He had no lunch to stare at, so he stared at the eraser. It looked like a perfectly normal pink pencil eraser.

Obviously, it wasn't. It was magic.

Carson's eyes turned to his pants. The stain was still there. He wanted it gone, and the solution seemed to be in his hand. But again, he was scared.

What if he rubbed the stain three times and more than the stain disappeared? What if his pants disappeared? What if his legs disappeared?

Was that a risk he was willing to take?

"Go for it, dude," Riley said. Riley was munching on fish sticks when she said this, so it was very possible that she didn't give the best advice.

"Easy for you to say," Carson whispered. "It's not your pants we're talking about. Or, you know, the lower half of your body."

Riley nodded and took another bite. "So we test it out on some other things," she said.

It was a good idea, but they went about it all wrong. Instead of staining a napkin with ketchup and seeing if the eraser would remove the stain, Riley tried something else first.

She snatched the eraser from Carson. And before Carson knew what was happening, his butt was hitting the ground.

"Oww!" Carson yelped from the floor.

"Holy macaroni!" Riley said with a laugh. "It worked on your chair. So cool!"

"Of course it worked on my chair," Carson said as he stood up. Rubbing his lower back, he surveyed the cafetorium. No one seemed to notice what had happened.

No one, that is, except Hunter Barnes.

Hunter didn't see the eraser make the chair disappear. He only saw the aftermath.

But that was enough.

"Hey, everyone!" Hunter shouted as he pointed. "Carson is falling on his butt for some reason! Is it because he had another accident in his PANTS? Seems like the only possible answer!"

Carson snatched the eraser back from Riley and said, "Great. Now we have to get outta here, too."

"Where are we going?"

"To the Dungeon."

Chapter Twelve

THE DUNGEON

The bathroom in the basement of Hopewell Elementary had been called the Dungeon for as long as anyone could remember. And if Locker 37 was the most amazing thing in the known universe, then the Dungeon was possibly the most depressing.

The Dungeon was rarely used, which is usually good for a bathroom. It usually means the place is in tip-top shape.

The Dungeon was *not* in tip-top shape. The fixtures on the sinks were rusty. Large, dark, butterfly-shaped stains marked the porcelain. The lights flickered. And there was always a dripping sound, but it was impossible to locate its source.

Carson had never been in the Dungeon. He had only heard stories about desperate kids who had rushed in with their hands on their zippers and rushed out with terrified looks on their faces. These stories were always told in whispers that made them sound like near-death experiences.

"I'm lucky I made it outta there alive," kids would basically say.

Carson was willing to risk death today, because he knew the Dungeon was probably the most private place in the school. But . . .

"I can't go in there!" Riley screamed as she stood at the door to the Dungeon.

"Don't be scared," Carson said.

"I'm not scared," Riley said. "I'm a girl."

The Dungeon didn't have urinals or a sign that indicated it was a boys' bathroom, but because of its decrepit condition, everyone assumed it was.

Carson knew it didn't matter whether girls went into boys' bathrooms or boys went into girls' bathrooms. In fact, half the restaurants in town had bathrooms that anyone was allowed to go in. Riley was just making an excuse. But he could understand that. It's hard to admit you're scared.

"Fine," he said. "You stand guard at the door. I'll go in there, take off my pants, try the eraser, and if my pants disappear, then I'll call for you."

"I'm definitely not going in there if you're pantless!" Riley said.

"You don't have to go in," Carson said. "Just find Bryce Dodd. He loves wearing shorts, but he hates cold weather. So he puts jeans on over his shorts every chilly morning, and then he takes the jeans off at lunch when the weather starts to get warm."

"Huh," Riley said. "That's . . . weird."

"Bryce is weird," Carson said. "But he's also nice. Tell him I need to borrow his jeans and he'll give them to you. I can stay in the Dungeon if I need to. No one will bother me in here."

"If that's what you think is the best plan," Riley said.

It *was* the best plan, because it was Carson's only plan.

He nodded, took a deep breath, and stepped through the door and into the Dungeon.

Chapter Thirteen
UNLUCKY

The Dungeon was worse than Carson had imagined.

The smell of mold was overpowering.

The mirrors were all cracked, and so when Carson caught a glimpse of his reflection, it looked like his face had been taken apart and clumsily put back together.

The drip was not the only sound that

echoed through the room. There was a high-pitched squeal coming from above. Muffled scream? The cry of a ghost? It was hard to tell. All Carson knew was that he wanted to get this over with.

He hurried to a stall in the back corner and pulled its door shut. The walls of the stall were covered in strange graffiti that said things like:

Greta Hallowell Is Still Invisible

Try Not to Trust Zero Gravity

Flush The Toilet + U Will B Sucked into the Burrito Dimension!

Carson didn't understand what any of these things meant, but they made him nervous. For a naturally nervous kid in an exceedingly nerve-racking situation, he didn't exactly need that. He wanted to be done with this and move on.

So as fast as he could, he pulled his pants off. He almost fell over, but he had the graffiti-stained wall there to brace his body against.

Once his pants were off, he wasn't sure where to put them. The floor was too grimy. It would simply add more stains. And if there was ever a hook on the door, it had been removed years ago.

He didn't want the pants touching his body when he rubbed them with the eraser. So he had only one option.

The toilet.

The toilet tank was old, but it was the cleanest thing around.

He draped the pants over the tank and crouched down, holding the eraser in front of the stain. He crossed his fingers and closed his eyes.

Then he rubbed.

Three times.

The drip and the high-pitched squeal were now replaced by the sound of rushing water.

Whoosh!

And Carson's face was suddenly wet.

He opened his eyes to find the toilet tank was gone.

His pants were still there, and still stained. But they were now floating on top of a geyser of water that was shooting up from where the toilet tank had been.

Uh-oh.

He shouldn't have closed his eyes.

Because Carson had rubbed the toilet tank instead of the pants.

Chapter Fourteen
THE FLOOD

The water shooting from the toilet was covering the floor, and Carson had no choice but to run. He had to leave his pants behind. They were soaked, anyway. There was no

•72•

way he could wear them now.
Less than an inch of water
had collected on the floor
when Carson ran for the exit, but it felt
like he was fleeing a tidal wave. And as he

broke out into the basement hallway, he screamed, "Take cover!"

"Holy penne rigate!" Riley yelled. "Where are your pants?"

"It's not important," he said. "We've gotta go. Now!"

"Wait, wait, wait," Riley said as she held up a hand. "Before we go anywhere, answer me this one question: Does your underwear have MONDAY written on it?"

Monday wasn't *written* on it. It was *stitched* on it.

Carson's father had bought him underwear for every day of the week. Carson had nearly a month's worth of underwear like this: four pairs of Mondays, four pairs of Tuesdays, and so on. His father believed it made getting

dressed in the morning easier because it narrowed down the choices. But what it obviously ended up doing was embarrassing his son.

Carson's face turned bright red and he mumbled, "Undergarments are unimportant right now. We gotta move."

That's when the water came spilling through the crack under the door to the Dungeon. And Carson didn't need to say another word. Riley bolted. And Carson followed.

There was nowhere else to hide in the basement.

All the doors were locked. So Riley led Carson to a stairway that climbed toward the back of the gym.

"If we go that way, I have to cut across the gym!" Carson cried. "In the middle of a class. In my underwear!"

"You mean in your Monday undies," Riley reminded him. "Sorry, but this is our best option. Because if we go the way we came in, we'll end up near the teachers' lounge, and we're sure to get in trouble then. Plus, I have the perfect plan to sneak you into the equipment room, where you can wait until I find Bryce Dodd and his jeans."

"Okay, so what do we need to do?" Carson asked.

"Gimme the eraser," she said.

"What?" Carson said, holding the eraser tight to his chest. "No. Not after what you did to me at lunch."

"I'm sorry that I do hilarious things," Riley said. "But I also do very smart things. You're gonna have to trust me. We're running out of time."

It wasn't an exaggeration. They were standing at the bottom of the stairway, and the hall was quickly filling up with water.

"Fine," Carson said, and he handed Riley the eraser. "You better know what you're doing."

"I always do," Riley said as she hopped up the stairs. "Wait here."

Chapter Fifteen

UP A ROPE

The water was up to the first stair and it was coming faster every second.

Carson climbed up to the fifth stair to stay dry. He wasn't sure what was making him more nervous: the water or not knowing what Riley was doing with the eraser.

She had told him to wait there, but he couldn't do it. Even though he trusted Riley, he knew her love of mischief often influenced her decisions. He would risk being spotted in his underwear if it meant he could keep an eye on her.

So Carson climbed to the top of the stairs, which led to a short hallway and a door that opened into the back of the gym. When he got on his tippy-toes, he could peer through a window in the door and see what was happening.

The gym was full of second-graders practicing gymnastics. There were kids on balance beams, others on parallel bars, and one trying to figure out the pommel horse. None of them seemed to notice Riley, who was climbing a rope in the middle of the gym.

The higher she got, the more worried Carson got.

What was she going to do?

What if Mr. Trundle, the gym teacher, saw her?

How was she possibly going to distract everyone in the gym so that it was safe for Carson to run to the equipment room?

When Riley was near the top of the rope, she held on with one hand while holding the eraser with the other.

Below, the second-graders jumped and tumbled.

Above, Riley lifted the eraser and rubbed something on the ceiling.

Then she climbed a little higher and reached her arm up into a hole in the ceiling that she had just created.

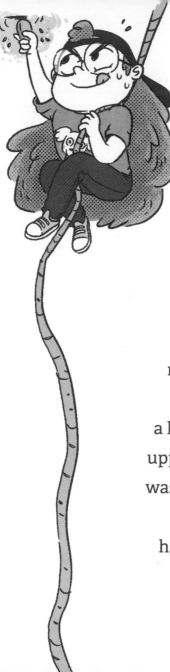

Carson thought she might be making the lightbulbs disappear. It would be a clever way to make the gym dark enough for Carson to sneak through undetected.

But all lights remained on.

And Riley climbed a little higher, until the upper half of her body was hidden in the ceiling.

And that's when it happened.

The unthinkable.

It started raining cockroaches.

As in . . . COCKROACHES!

And not just any cockroaches. Giant Madagascar hissing cockroaches.

Chapter Sixteen

THE "WAIT A MINUTE, IS THIS A HISTORY CHAPTER?" CHAPTER

You want to know about the cockroaches, right?

Of course you do.

We'll get to that. Promise. But first, some history.

Hopewell Elementary School wasn't always an elementary school. In fact, it was once a random collection of neutrons, protons, electrons, antielectrons, photons, and neutrinos floating around outer space in the seconds after the big bang.

Okay, to be fair, we were all a random collection of neutrons, protons, electrons, antielectrons, photons, and neutrinos floating around outer space in the seconds after the big bang.

Let's talk about more recent history. Like 13.7 billion years or so later.

Long after the big bang, long after our sun and solar system and Earth were formed, and long after the age of dinosaurs, there was a forest. And in that forest, there was a hole in the ground.

The hole glowed a beautiful orange and seemed to have no bottom. But if you dropped something into the hole, it always shot right back out, like popcorn popping out of hot oil.

Animals would come to the hole whenever they were thirsty or hungry or afraid. And somehow, some way, whatever they wanted would appear.

If a bear wanted blueberries, then a bush would bloom behind him.

If a fox wanted a drink, a trickle of water would slide down from some leaves above and fall into her mouth.

If a duck wanted a friend, another duck would suddenly show up, flapping and quacking in delight.

This hole was a wonderful and magical

hole. And it performed its magic every day.

Until an adult found it.

This adult was foolish, as adults often are. He didn't like wonderful, glowing holes in the ground, for some reason. So when he came upon it, he covered the hole with a big flat stone. Then he covered that stone with another stone. He kept stacking stones upon stones until he had made the foundation for a house.

He built a house upon that foundation and he lived in that house for many years. But the hole didn't give him anything he wanted because magical glowing holes won't do that if you're foolish enough to cover them up.

The house stood for a long time, long after the adult died. During those many years, other adults with axes and saws cut down the forest around the house. They built roads around the house, as well as farms and stores. The place that was once a forest eventually became a town.

But they didn't have a school. So the town turned the house into a one-room schoolhouse. Years went by. The population grew. So they added to the schoolhouse.

It became a two-room schoolhouse.

Then a four-room schoolhouse.

Then eight. Then sixteen.

Then they couldn't add anything more.

It was easier to start over.

HOPEWELL ELEMENTARY

They tore it all down and built a big school in its place. But they didn't move the stone that covered the hole. In fact, they poured concrete over it.

The big school served every student in town from kindergarten to twelfth grade. They called it the Hopewell School, because, well, they hoped everything went well there. And it did, for the most part.

They built four hundred lockers in the school, one for every student. One of those lockers was Locker 37. But it was a regular locker back then.

The population kept growing. The school was not big enough for all of the students. So they built a middle school and a high school at the other end of town.

This is when the Hopewell School became Hopewell Elementary. It was a very important moment in the history of the universe.

On the first day that it was officially named Hopewell Elementary, there was an assembly. The fourth-graders piled into the cafetorium, where the music teacher gave them the lyrics to the new school song. It was their job to learn the song and teach it to the younger students. The song went as follows:

At Hopewell Elementary
We're all put to the test.
Living our lives honorably
We're kind to every guest.
We fill the world with harmony.
We never, ever rest.
At Hopewell Elementary
We always try our best.

The music teacher taught the fourth-graders to sing the last line as loud as they could and to stomp after the last three words. The fourth-graders happily did as taught, because being loud and stomping is something fourth-graders are quite good at. In fact, they stomped so hard that it shook the floor beneath the cafetorium.

The shaking floor shook the school's foundation, which caused the concrete to crack in a spot directly below a hallway full of lockers.

That crack spread to the rock that covered the hole.

Orange light snuck through the crack.

And *(cue some glorious music!)* magic returned to the spot for the first time in a long time.

Therefore, when a girl named Charlotte Dover opened her locker later that same morning, she found an infinitely regenerating peanut butter and jelly sandwich inside, which solved her problem: She had forgotten her lunch and had no lunch money.

Her locker was, you guessed it: Locker 37.

From that day forward, the fourth-graders knew about Locker 37. But they kept the secret to themselves, as all fourth-graders in the future would agree to do.

To everyone else, Hopewell Elementary seemed entirely normal.

It had a playground with a rock in the middle of it that kids sometimes tripped over.

It had an art room with a window that faced the sun, which would shine in the eyes of kids who were trying to paint pictures of bowls of fruit.

It had a giant terrarium, next to a heating vent, in a classroom above the gym.

What's a terrarium, you ask?

In simple terms, it's like an aquarium, but without the fish. Sometimes there are reptiles or amphibians in them. Sometimes spiders.

This particular terrarium, however, was full of Madagascar hissing cockroaches.

Chapter Seventeen

IN THE TERRARIUM

Madagascar hissing cockroaches are the biggest cockroaches in the world. Fully grown, they're more than two inches long. But they're not like the cockroaches so many people fear.

They don't hide in your walls and eat your garbage. They're vegetarians that enjoy fresh leaves for lunch.

They don't bite or sting or do anything

harmful. But they hiss when they're scared.

Until Riley made it disappear, the terrarium full of Madagascar hissing cockroaches was in Mrs. Rosenstein's classroom. Mrs. Rosenstein was the health teacher and an amateur entomologist, which is a fancy name for someone who's really into bugs. She loved beetles and honeybees, grasshoppers and praying mantises. But her favorite insects to study were Madagascar hissing cockroaches.

Riley knew that there was a vent in the ceiling of the gym, and that vent was below another vent that connected directly to Mrs. Rosenstein's classroom.

How did she know this? Because every

fourth-grader knew this.

Even if Mrs. Rosenstein wasn't their teacher, every kid would visit her classroom and meet the cockroaches by the time they reached fourth grade. And every kid who met the cockroaches would learn that the noise coming through the vents from the gym below would scare the cockroaches and make them hiss.

"They feel the same way about dodgeball that you do," Mrs. Rosenstein had joked one day when Riley was staring through the terrarium glass at the dozens of cockroaches.

"What would happen if they got out?" Riley asked.

"If there was no vent behind the

terrarium," Mrs. Rosenstein said, "I suppose they might fall into the gym."

"Wouldn't that hurt them?" Riley asked.

"They'd be fine," Mrs. Rosenstein said. "They don't have wings like other cockroaches. But they're just as tough. It might scare the gym class, though."

Chapter Eighteen

OPERATION COCKROACH RAIN

I t did scare the gym class. A few seconds after Riley erased the vents and the terrarium, the cockroaches started falling from above.

They hissed as they fell onto the mats, and they hissed as they fell into the hair of the

second-graders. They hissed as they scurried along the floor. They hissed as the children screamed.

"Wah!"

Hiss!

"Wahhh!"

Hiss!

"Wahhhhh!"

Hiss!

And Mr. Trundle, the gym teacher, shouted, "Run, children, run! The end of days is upon us!"

This was an overreaction. The end of days was not upon them. But the end of class was.

There was a stampede for the exit. In a matter of seconds,

the gym was empty. Except for
Riley, of course, and the nearly
one hundred hissing cockroaches
that were now climbing
on the balance beam,
the uneven bars, and the
pommel horse.

Riley slid down the rope
and yelled, "Operation Cockroach Rain is
a success! The coast is clear, Carson! Move
your Monday undies that way!"

Then she pointed to the door in the
back that led to the equipment room.

Of all the ways she could have snuck
Carson through the gym, this is the one
Riley chose? A rain of cockroaches?

It shouldn't have surprised Carson.
Riley always found the most ridiculous

solutions to problems. But she always found solutions.

She was strangely brilliant. And brilliantly strange.

Carson opened the door slowly and took a few steps into the gym. A minefield of cockroaches lay in front of him. He didn't love cockroaches, but he definitely didn't want to squish any.

So he tiptoed over the gym mats, whispering "shoo, shoo, shoo," as he went. But the cockroaches didn't shoo. Instead, they started climbing his bare legs.

"This. Was. A. Terrible. Plan," Carson

 said through clenched teeth as the cockroaches brushed their antennae against his skin, tickling his knee.

"Settle down, roach magnet," Riley said. "They're harmless."

"If they're so harmless then you should scoop them all up and bring them back to Mrs. Rosenstein," Carson said as he gently nudged one off his thigh with the backs of his fingers.

"No time for that. I'm off to find Bryce and his jeans," Riley said as she tossed Carson the eraser.

It bounced once on the floor... twice... and then... Carson caught it.

"Careful," Carson said. "What if the floor disappeared?"

Riley shrugged him off. "It didn't, so who cares? Stop with the what-ifs and go hide. I'm off to get those jeans."

No amount of begging and pleading could keep Riley there in the gym with Carson. And by the time she was through the exit, his bare legs were covered in cockroaches.

Using the eraser on them would've been too dangerous. If he slipped, he could possibly erase himself. So instead, he screamed, "Get off of me!" and he shook his body like he was a wet dog.

Cockroaches flew in all directions and landed on the floor unharmed. They started to skitter back toward Carson.

He leaped forward.

And leaped again.

And again.

Hopping from spot to spot, careful not to land on any cockroaches, until he had made it all the way to the equipment room.

Once he was inside, he slammed the door shut.

Chapter Nineteen
IN THE DARK

It was so dark in the equipment room that Carson couldn't see the walls. He didn't know where the light switch was. He was worried that if he stumbled through the darkness pawing for it, he'd trip over a hockey stick or a tennis racket and sprain his ankle.

So he sat down on the floor. And he waited.

He was so disappointed in himself.

If he had only used the eraser on the stain as soon as he pulled it out of Locker 37, he wouldn't be hiding pantless in a dark equipment room. He'd be in math class right now. Even if they were multiplying fractions, which he still didn't understand, he'd much rather be there.

His breath quickened. His heart thumped. He felt a tear slip down his face. Then another. Then more than he could count.

That's when light poured into the room. Someone had opened the door.

A figure stood in the doorway.

"Is someone in here?" a voice asked.

It was a boy's voice. It was familiar.

"Ye . . . ye . . . yes," Carson stuttered between sobs.

"Well, get outta here!" the voice said. "There's a totally amazing flood going on in the basement and I want to see how many rubber balls I can make float in it."

That's when Carson could place the voice. And that's when the lights came on in the closet.

Hunter Barnes stood next to the light switch.

Out of instinct, Carson jumped to his feet.

And out of instinct, Hunter began to laugh.

Chapter Twenty

OH NO

"You're crying!" Hunter shouted. "In your undies! I've gotta tell everyone. This is the greatest day ever!"

It was the opposite for Carson. It was the worst day he could possibly imagine. And his feelings suddenly changed from humiliation to anger. His grip on the eraser tightened.

"Get out of here," Carson growled.

"No way, no how," Hunter said. "Not until I get a picture first. I don't have a phone. Do you have a phone I can borrow so I can take a picture of you crying in your undies and then share it with everyone?"

Even if he did have a phone, which he didn't, Carson would never, under any circumstances, let Hunter borrow it. And for Hunter to ask at this moment was beyond insulting.

"Leave!" Carson yelled, and without even thinking about it, he raised the eraser.

"Is that your phone?" Hunter asked. "It's small. And pink. Do you have a pink flip phone, Carson? Because that would be so funny."

Carson couldn't take it anymore. A sound came out of his mouth that was sort of a scream and sort of a howl. And totally frightening.

It was the sound of a wild animal.

He sprinted toward Hunter. Before Hunter knew what was happening, Carson was rubbing his face with the eraser.

One time.

Two times.

Three times.

Pop.

Hunter was gone.

Chapter Twenty-One

BRYCE'S JEANS

This was not good. Carson was disgusted with himself.

Hunter was mean. Hunter was cruel. Hunter was not Carson's friend. But did Hunter deserve to be . . . erased?

"Whoa," someone said. "What did you do, Carson?"

That someone was Bryce Dodd.

He was standing in the gym, near the

entrance to the equipment room. He was wearing shorts. He was holding out a pair of jeans.

"I can explain," Carson said, stepping into the light.

"You . . . you . . . you made Hunter disappear . . . with an eraser?" Bryce said as he took a step back.

Carson was still holding the eraser up and he realized how threatening that might appear. So he lowered it and said, "It's a magic eraser. I found it in Locker 37. Locker 37 provides solutions to fourth-graders' problems. I swear. It's the truth. I have a note and everything. Or, I had a note. It was in my pants. And my pants had a stain . . . It's a long story."

"I believe you," Bryce said.

"You do?" Carson said.

"Um, yeah," Bryce said. "I did just watch you rub Hunter's face with that eraser and you made him disappear, so I'm sorta willing to believe anything."

"Oh," Carson said. "Good."

"Just tell me that you're not, like, an evil wizard or something," Bryce whispered.

"I can promise you I'm not an evil wizard," Carson said. "Or else why would I need to borrow your jeans?"

It was a good point. Conjuring a pair of jeans would be well within an evil wizard's abilities.

Bryce smiled at the joke. Then he stepped forward, handed Carson the jeans, and said, "Riley told me you needed them. And I'm happy to help out. But just so you know, it's supposed to be warm later. These jeans might make you a bit sweaty. That's why I prefer shorts."

"Thanks, but I don't exactly have a lot of wardrobe options at the moment," Carson said as he started to pull the jeans on.

"Oh, cool," Bryce said, pointing at Carson's underwear. "They have the day of the week sewn onto them. That must make getting dressed in the mornings so much easier."

Carson didn't respond. He zipped up, sighed in relief, and asked, "So where's Riley?"

"Math," Bryce said. "Mrs. Shen told her she had to stay. But I got a bathroom pass. Mrs. Shen said if I saw you or Hunter that I should bring you back to class. Since it's the first day, she thinks you might've gotten lost on your way back from lunch."

Lost? Really? Mrs. Shen should've known that fourth-graders never get lost.

Well . . . except for Hunter. Where the heck did he go when he was erased?

"Okay," Carson said. "I'll go with you. But we really need to find out what happened to Hunter. I shouldn't have done what I did."

"It was a mistake I'm sure we can fix," Bryce said as he turned around to head out of the gym.

"But I think we've got another problem to deal with first."

It was a problem Carson should have predicted, but didn't.

Because he had forgotten about the cockroaches.

And he had forgotten about the water.

But you better believe he remembered both now.

A door busted open, the same door that led to the hall that led to the stairs that led to the basement where the Dungeon and its broken toilet was.

A wave of water gushed forth.

And the cockroaches were riding that wave like a hundred insect surfers.

Chapter Twenty-Two

WET

Bryce and Carson were nearly knocked over by the wave. By

the time they found their balance, the water was up to their shins, and the cockroaches were swimming all around them.

"See," Bryce said, pointing down at the dry fabric above his bare knees. "Shorts are where it's at."

"Not for long," Carson said. "This water is gonna keep coming and coming."

"So erase it," Bryce said.

Could he? Was water erasable?

Everything else seemed to be. Why not give it a try?

There was only one problem. When the wave hit Carson's legs, he dropped the eraser.

"I don't have the eraser!" Carson shouted.

"Is this it?" Bryce asked, reaching down into the water and holding up something orangish and eraser-shaped.

"No," Carson said, stepping back. "That's a cockroach."

"Oh," Bryce said, examining it closely and noticing its legs. He dropped it and reached down again. "How about this?"

"Nope," Carson said, taking another step back. "Another cockroach."

"Oh," Bryce said again, examining this one closely, too. "They're cute little buggies, aren't they?"

Carson didn't exactly agree, but he had to find the eraser. That meant sifting through the cockroaches, cute or not. And in the water, they all looked like erasers.

So he stuck his hand down in and pulled something up.

Another cockroach.

He didn't want to put it back in the water and end up grabbing it again, so he showed it to Bryce.

"Do you mind holding this?" he said. "I mean, you did say they were cute."

"Sure," Bryce said. "Put it anywhere on me."

That's exactly what Carson did. He placed the cockroach on Bryce's shoulder and kept searching.

He picked up another cockroach, then another, and another. He placed each of them on Bryce's body.

Bryce smiled and said, "Keep 'em coming!"

As Carson said earlier, Bryce was weird. But nice.

It wasn't until Bryce was almost entirely covered in cockroaches and the water was up to the boys' thighs that Carson found the eraser.

"Phew!" he said, wiping his brow. Then he reached down and rubbed the water with it once, twice, three . . .

Pop.

Everything, including his borrowed jeans, was now dry.

"Cool!" Bryce said. "Let's go."

"How about we leave those things behind first?" Carson replied.

There were so many cockroaches on Bryce that his skin was barely visible. He didn't see what the big deal was. But he stood there for a very long time, trying to consider the other perspective.

"Fine," he finally said with a sigh. "But you're going to have to break the bad news to my little friends."

Chapter Twenty-Three
MATH CLASS

Bryce carried the cockroaches to Mr. Trundle's office and hid them in the drawers of his desk. Then the boys zipped down to the basement and the Dungeon. The water wasn't flowing from the broken toilet anymore, but Carson turned a knob behind the toilet to shut the water off anyway. Finally, they sprinted to math class.

As they stumbled through the door, Mrs. Shen said, "Thank you for joining us."

"I'm sorry I'm late," Carson said. "There were bathroom . . . problems."

The entire class laughed. Except for Riley. She cringed.

"It's the first day, so I'll cut you some slack," Mrs. Shen said. "Any sign of Hunter Barnes out there?"

"Seems to have disappeared," Bryce said. And then he said, "Ouch!"

The reason he said, "Ouch!" was because Carson stepped on his foot. Carson didn't like to lie, but this was not the sort of truth he wanted to share.

"You're fourth-graders now," Mrs. Shen told them. "That means you have to accept more responsibilities than ever before. You're the leaders of this school. You set the example for the younger children. Which means doing your best to show up on time."

"Yes, ma'am," Carson said as he took a seat next to Riley.

"I'll tell Hunter the same thing when he arrives," Mrs. Shen said. "But for now, let's talk about math. Everyone here knows how to multiply fractions, right?"

Wrong.

Carson had somehow passed a few tests in third grade that were about multiplying fractions, but he didn't remember how to do it. So he sank low in his chair, hoping Mrs. Shen wouldn't invite him up to the whiteboard for a demonstration.

"You got the pants?" Riley whispered to him.

"Yes, thank you," Carson whispered back. "But I sorta . . . kinda . . . erased . . . Hunter."

"Holy tagliolini!" Riley shouted. "What?"

"Riley," Mrs. Shen said, "if you're having trouble hearing, you can sit in the front of the class. And you should know to put your hand up first before asking questions."

"Yes, ma'am," Riley said.

"To answer your question," Mrs. Shen said, "I was asking the class what you get when you multiply two-thirds times three-quarters."

"Six-twelfths," Bryce said.

"Can someone simplify that?" she asked.

"He only said, like, two words," Riley replied. "How much simpler can you get?"

"True enough, Riley, but *simplification* is a term for making fractions as clear as possible," Mrs. Shen explained. "You probably covered it last year."

Alisha Reddy raised her hand and said, "Six-twelfths can be simplified as one-half."

"One hundred percent, positively,

absolutely correct," Mrs. Shen said.

Carson would have to take her word for it.

Meanwhile, it gave Riley an idea.

"Pass me the eraser," she whispered to Carson.

"I'm not dealing with any more cockroaches," Carson whispered back.

"It's not like that. I only need it for a second and I'm not about to make anything disappear."

Riley was Carson's best friend, and even though she often made him anxious, she rarely lied to him. On the other hand, this was a powerful object, and Riley had a history of not necessarily abusing power, but having a bit too much fun with it.

"I think it's best if I hold on to the eraser," he whispered.

"That is, if you can hold on to it," Riley said. Which she followed up with a, "Think fast!"

Before he realized what was happening, Carson was catching an egg that Riley had thrown at him. To catch it, he had to drop the eraser.

The eraser bounced off his desk . . . and right into Riley's clutches.

"Sweeeeet," Riley whispered. "That worked even better than I expected."

"Why would you even have an egg?" he asked.

She shrugged. "Because you never know when you'll need to throw one."

Then she broke the eraser in half.

Carson put his hand over his mouth to stop the gasp, and whispered through his fingers, "You didn't."

"I did," she whispered as she handed him back one of the halves. "Now we both have one."

This was a fraction that he understood. But was a half as good as a whole?

With both objects hidden under his desk, Carson rubbed the egg three times with his half of the eraser.

Pop.

The entire egg disappeared.

Chapter Twenty-Four

THE "COME ON, THIS ISN'T ANOTHER MATH CHAPTER, IS IT?" CHAPTER

I t is.

It is another math chapter.

Don't worry, this one is exciting. Not like that last math chapter, which was really confusing and boring, right?

Why is this one exciting? Because it's about breaking erasers in half! Just try to put the book down now! You can't, can you?

The big question posed in this chapter is: How do you turn 1 eraser into 32 erasers?

The short answer is: Break that eraser into 32 erasers that are $\frac{1}{32}$ the size of the original.

But how does one do that?

Well, it takes five steps. Simple multiplication of some fractions will do the trick. Check it out:

1. If you have 1 eraser and break it in half ($\frac{1}{2}$), then you end up with 2 erasers that are equal in size. That's exactly what Carson and Riley did. But you know this already. Because you're smart. You might even be the smartest kid in your school. It's certainly not impossible.

2. Now that you, possibly the smartest kid in your school, have 2 smaller erasers of equal size, you're going to break each of those small erasers in half. Breaking a half in half is the same as multiplying ½ times ½. Each ½ is a fraction. If you're like Carson, you might not know how to multiply fractions. Don't worry. It's easy. Multiply the top numbers of the fraction together and the bottom numbers of the fraction together. In this case, you multiply 1 times 1 and get . . . 1! Then 2 times 2 gets you . . . 4! You put the 1 on top and the 4 on the bottom, and now you have ¼. Otherwise known as 1 out of 4. Otherwise known as a quarter. That's right. You've got 4 magic

erasers now, and each one is ¼ the size of the original. See, easy!

$$\frac{1}{2} \times \frac{1}{2} = \frac{1}{4}$$

3. Your teacher might tell you that the top number of a fraction is called the *numerator* and the bottom number of a fraction is called the *denominator*. But those names are too confusing, don't you think? Let's just call them the Topsy and the Bottomsy. So now we have 4 erasers and each one is ¼ the size of the original eraser. Let's break them each in half again. In other words, let's multiply ¼ and ½. Remember, multiply the Topsies (1×1) and the Bottomsies (2×4) and you'll

TOPSY

$$\frac{1}{4}$$

BOTTOMSY

end up with ⅛. That's 8 erasers that are ⅛ the size of the original.

$$\frac{1}{2} \times \frac{1}{4} = \frac{1}{8}$$

4. Pop quiz: What's ⅛ times ½ ? If you said $\frac{1}{16}$, then you're right. It's also becoming increasingly likely that you are indeed the smartest kid in your school. You're also a kid with 16 erasers that are $\frac{1}{16}$ the size of the original eraser.

$$\frac{1}{2} \times \frac{1}{8} = \frac{1}{16}$$

5. We're at step five, where we're breaking the eraser in half for the fifth time. Of course that means we're taking our fractions

($\frac{1}{16}$ and $\frac{1}{2}$) and multiplying our Topsies (1×1) and our Bottomsies (16×2) and ending up with $\frac{1}{32}$. 32 erasers that are $\frac{1}{32}$ the size of the first eraser. If the original eraser is about the size of a Madagascar hissing cockroach, then the 32 smaller erasers are pretty small, probably about the size of an eraser you find at the end of a pencil. It would be hard to break them up any more.

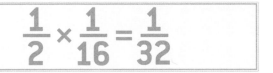

$$\frac{1}{2} \times \frac{1}{16} = \frac{1}{32}$$

6. But what if we had a really, really big eraser that we could keep breaking in half, over and over again? How many times would we have to break the pieces in half to

give every person in the world a magic eraser?

7. 33 times. There are approximately 7,600,000,000 (or 7.6 billion) people in the world, and to make sure each person gets a magic eraser, we'd have to break the original eraser in half once and then keep breaking each smaller piece in half 32 times.

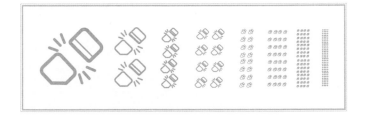

8. If you don't believe it, do the arithmetic. Your Topsy will remain 1, because 1 times 1 will always be 1, no matter how many

times you multiply it. And your Bottomsy will keep doubling. In other words, it will be the result of: 2×2×2×2×2×2×2×2×2×2×2 ×2×2×2×2×2×2×2×2×2×2×2 ×2×2×2×2×2×2×2×2×2×2. This is also known as 2 to the 33rd power, which is an exponential equation. And, yes, it is very, very, very powerful. But you probably don't have to worry about knowing that stuff until you're older.

$$2\times2\times2\times2\times2\times2\times2\times2\times2\times2\times2\times2\times2$$
$$\times2\times2\times2\times2\times2\times2\times2\times2\times2\times2\times2\times2\times$$
$$2\times2\times2\times2\times2\times2\times2\times2$$
$$= 2^{33}$$
$$= 8{,}589{,}934{,}592$$

9. There's blank space here to the right of the page where you're free to work on your arithmetic (especially if you find this book in the library!). Or you're welcome to find the universe's biggest eraser and keep breaking the pieces in half until you have at least 8,589,934,592 pieces that are $\frac{1}{8,589,934,592}$ the size of the original.

$$8{,}589{,}934{,}592 - 7{,}600{,}000{,}000$$
$$= 989{,}934{,}592$$

10. That leaves you with 989,934,592 extra erasers after you've given one to every human. Feel free to distribute them to any narwhals, platypuses, and aye-ayes.

11. That might take a while, though.

Chapter Twenty-Five

32 IS THE MAGIC NUMBER

It was time for recess.

All but one of the kids in fourth grade gathered on the playground in front of Hopewell Elementary. Hunter Barnes was the missing one.

Carson and Riley were standing by a willow tree at the back of the playground. And they were doing something they never did. They were arguing.

"You told me that Locker 37 would solve any problem, right?" Riley said. "Our biggest problem now is that Hunter Barnes vanished into thin air, right?"

"Exactly," Carson said. "But it was caused by the eraser. And now we have two erasers. Won't that cause more problems?"

"Unless Locker 37 wants to give us another solution, I think the eraser is it," Riley said. "And the more erasers, the better. Wouldn't you agree?"

"I would not," Carson said. "And I really think we should check the locker again before you jump to any more conclusions."

"Fine."

Since the recess monitors rarely

worried about kids sneaking back *into* school, it meant Carson and Riley could slip inside virtually undetected.

They hurried to Locker 37.

They opened it.

There was a faint orange glow in the locker, but otherwise . . . ?

Nothing.

"Oh well," someone said behind them.

It was Bryce, but he wasn't the only one there. He was followed by a few dozen other kids.

"What the heck is going on?" Carson asked.

"Another thing you told me was that we were supposed to spread the word about Locker 37 to every fourth-grader," Riley said. "Well, Bryce has been spreading the word, and I guess these are the ones who were smart and brave enough to sneak away from recess."

There were more than thirty fourth-graders gathered in the hall around Locker 37. It wasn't all the fourth-graders, but it was plenty of them.

"Thanks for coming, everyone," Riley said. "Right now you are standing in front of Locker 37, which is a completely magical locker that provides solutions to problems. Today's problem is that Hunter Barnes is missing."

"Good!" Violet Simpson shouted.

"No, it's bad," Riley said. "Because even though Hunter can be mean sometimes, he's also one of us. A fourth-grader. And we have to stick together."

"You can say that again!" Darlene Waterford shouted.

"I *will* say that again," Riley said. "We fourth-graders have to stick together! Which means that everyone here will get a piece of what Locker 37 gave us. We'll use them to search this school inside and out. And together we will find Hunter Barnes."

"What did Locker 37 give you?" Kenny Cho asked.

Riley held up her eraser. Then she walked over to the janitor closet, which was still missing the doorknob and held shut by a wad of toilet paper. She rubbed the door three times with the eraser. The door disappeared.

The crowd gasped.

Then she pulled out a roll of toilet paper. She rubbed it with the eraser three times. It disappeared.

The crowd gasped.

Finally, she lowered the eraser toward the floor.

"Don't!" they all shouted.

She didn't.

But she got her point across.

"Everyone will get a magic eraser that makes things disappear," she said. Then Riley broke her eraser in half and handed a piece to Bryce.

Bryce broke his piece in half and handed half to a girl named Rosie, who broke her piece in half and handed half to a guy named Rajib. Then Bryce broke his piece again. And so did Riley. And so did

Rosie. And so did Rajib.

Carson watched in horror.

Before he knew it, there were sixteen other erasers in the hands of sixteen kids. But there were at least sixteen kids who didn't have erasers.

The small pieces were as small as they could get. Carson's half of the original eraser was the only thing left that could be broken.

Dozens of eyes stared at him. Carson was outnumbered, and fearing that he might face the same fate as Hunter, he surrendered.

"This is such a bad idea," he said, and he broke his piece in half.

A few moments later, there were thirty-two magic erasers in thirty-two kids' hands.

You already know how many times the erasers needed to be broken in half before everyone got one, right?

Or did you skip Chapter Twenty-Four?

Chapter Twenty-Six

MAYBE THIS WASN'T THE BEST IDEA . . .

The other fourth-graders had to test the erasers out. How could they resist?

Some of them returned to recess, while a few others stayed inside the school to commit acts of mischief.

Near the front steps, Patrick Huang rubbed the NO SKATEBOARDING sign with his eraser. It disappeared, and he hooted in celebration. Without the sign, skateboarding on school grounds became perfectly legal. At least that was the logic Patrick used.

On the playground, Didi DeBois used her eraser to get rid of a rock that she had tripped over ten minutes before. "Take that, you dastardly rock," she said with an evil laugh as she made it disappear.

Meanwhile, inside the school, Becky Niles distracted the cafeteria workers by making all the trash cans disappear. Not the trash, just the cans.

As the workers scrambled to bag up all the half-eaten apples and sandwich crusts, June Marcus snuck into the school's freezer and made the year's supply of frozen fish sticks disappear.

Both girls were immediately declared the school's greatest heroines.

Things were disappearing everywhere. Mostly small things that didn't cause too much of a fuss. Nothing that would make the teachers, staff, or younger students suspect there were magic erasers going around. Not even the fish sticks.

It was relatively harmless, but that didn't mean it wasn't going to soon get out of hand. And there was one thing that bothered Carson more than anything.

No one seemed to care about finding Hunter Barnes.

"And why did we give them all erasers, again?" he asked Riley. "How is this making things better?"

"We're fighting fire with fire," she said.

"That doesn't make any sense," Carson said. "Fire and fighting have nothing to do with finding Hunter Barnes."

Riley shrugged and said, "Well, at least it's fun."

It wasn't fun for Carson.

He wished that he had never found the note about Locker 37. He definitely wished that he had never let Riley start breaking the eraser in half.

If only he could get rid of them all. If only . . .

Wait a second.

Chapter Twenty-Seven
HE COULD!

He could get rid of them! He could use his eraser to erase all the erasers!

But he knew it might not be easy. There were thirty-one other erasers, after all, and not everyone would give theirs up without a fight.

He started with Bryce, a kid who had literally given him the pants off his own body. Carson figured he'd listen to reason.

"Hey, Bryce," Carson said as they walked back toward school at the end of recess.

"Hey, Carson," Bryce said. "Guess what? I made a blade of grass disappear. Over there!"

Bryce pointed to a patch of lawn that contained thousands of blades of grass. If one of them had disappeared, there would be no way of telling.

"That's really cool, Bryce," Carson said with a forced smile. "But I've got a problem. Can I ask you for another favor?"

"Sure," Bryce said.

"Can I have your eraser back?" Carson asked, sticking out his hand.

Bryce's face dropped. "Really?" he said.

"But everyone has one. And I kinda like mine. I thought that maybe if I figured out a way to make half of a blade of grass disappear, then I would have a new environmentally friendly way to mow my lawn."

"That's a good thing, I guess," Carson said. "But you see, the erasers are a distraction. We really need to focus on finding Hunter Barnes. He has a family and everything, and they'll definitely miss him if he's, like, in another dimension or something."

"Yeah," Bryce said. "But then what about my lawn?"

"Isn't a person more important than your lawn?" Carson said.

"Yeah," Bryce said. "But I'm not asking

you to give me back my jeans, am I?"

"I sorta need them," Carson said. "You know, to cover my underwear."

Bryce made a fist around his eraser and said, "I tell you what. I'll hold on to the eraser, but if I find any clues about where Hunter is, I'll make sure not to erase them."

Then Bryce started to run.

Chapter Twenty-Eight
KEISHA JAMES

Bryce was fast. There was no way Carson could catch him. But it's not like he had to catch him. They were both going to the same art class.

When Carson arrived at art, Bryce was sitting in the corner, taking deep breaths. He had a hand in his pocket, and his eyes were locked on Carson. Carson started to walk up to him so he could beg him to

give the eraser back. That's when Keisha
James stepped into Carson's path.

"Buddy!" Keisha said. "These erasers
are the best thing in the history of the
whole entire universe! I'm going to keep
mine forever and ever, and nothing will

ever stand in my way again!"

It sounded like something a supervillain would say. But Keisha wasn't a supervillain. In fact, she was quite honest and honorable. But she was also quite competitive. She was an amazing athlete and student, maybe the best in the school. And she didn't want anyone to be better than her.

Once, in third grade, Carson had accidentally looked at her paper during a math test. Keisha didn't tell the teacher, but after class, she took Carson aside and said, "Carson, buddy, if you're going to cheat, don't be so obvious about it. And don't cheat off of me. I don't want to be implicated in your failure. Work harder. Study your fractions. Do like I do. You're

lucky I didn't turn you in, but don't go asking me for any other favors. Because I don't give people anything they don't deserve."

Carson assumed that this included magic erasers.

So if Carson couldn't get an eraser back from Bryce by asking, then he definitely couldn't get one back from Keisha.

Which meant there was only one option:

He'd have to steal them all back.

Chapter Twenty-Nine

A MASTER THIEF?

The art teacher, Mr. Rao, pulled the shades down over the windows, blocking out the bright sunlight.

"We can't have sun in everyone's eyes," he said. "Because for the first day of class, we are going to create pictures of the world's most beautiful model."

Everyone in the room was seated on stools next to easels. And everyone looked around, trying to figure out where this supermodel was hiding.

Mr. Rao smiled and said, "I'm talking about *you*. Today we'll be doing self-portraits."

"What's a self-portrait?" Bryce asked.

"It's like a selfie," Mr. Rao said. "Without a phone."

"Where are the mirrors, then?" Keisha said. "We have to see ourselves to draw ourselves."

"No phones, no mirrors," Mr. Rao said. "I want you to draw yourselves from memory. I want to see you as you see yourselves with your mind's eye. Use whatever materials you like. Paint. Clay. Pencils."

"Then you're gonna see a stick figure,"

Bryce said. "Because that's all I can draw."

The class laughed, including Mr. Rao.

Meanwhile, Carson was starting to crawl across the floor.

Why? To steal the erasers, obviously.

Carson had never stolen anything in his life. He didn't know how to start, so he started crawling.

At first, before the crawling, Carson thought he might pick his friends' pockets. But he didn't know how a person even picks a pocket. He had enough trouble slipping his hand in the pocket of his own jeans (well, Bryce's jeans).

And he certainly couldn't make their pants disappear. That would be . . . wrong.

So he changed his focus to their backpacks. Carson figured that some of his classmates must have hidden the erasers in their backpacks.

The backpacks were all stored in cubbies by the door. If Carson could make the backpacks disappear, then maybe everything inside them would disappear. And if he could only make the backpacks themselves disappear, then maybe Carson could keep erasing the things inside until he found and erased the tiny erasers.

But that would take time. And people would notice. So he needed to distract everyone. Since he didn't have cockroaches, his next best option was to crawl.

"What are you doing?" Riley whispered to Carson as he crawled past her.

"Shh!" he whispered back. "I'm on a mission."

His mission was to erase the window shades so that the sun would shine through the window and into everyone's eyes. And while his classmates couldn't see, Carson would run over to the backpacks and start the erasing.

No one said it was a good plan.

Of course, other kids noticed Carson crawling by them and they all gave him suspicious looks, but they didn't say anything.

Until he reached the windows, that is. That's when Keisha spoke up.

"Um . . . Mr. Rao?" she said. "How is Carson going to do a self-portrait when he's crawling around on the floor?"

Mr. Rao turned just as Carson was rubbing the shade the second time.

"Carson!" he hollered.

It scared Carson so much that he dropped his eraser. Again.

It bounced once and then rolled toward Mr. Rao's desk.

"What are you doing over there, son?" Mr. Rao asked. "And what did you just drop?"

"Nothing," Carson said. "And nothing."

But before Carson could grab it back, Mr. Rao had picked up the eraser.

He examined it. He sniffed it.

"Is this thing an eraser?" he asked.

"A magic eraser," Bryce told him.

His classmates glared at Bryce. Not that Mr. Rao would ever believe him, of course.

"If only this *were* a magic eraser," Mr. Rao said with a laugh. "Then maybe it would get rid of this sunburn I got yesterday at the beach."

Then, since he didn't know any better, Mr. Rao did something stupid.

He thought he was being funny when he rubbed the eraser on his sunburned forehead.

One time.

Two times.

But before he could rub it a third time, Carson jumped to his feet and ran across the room.

And that's how he ended up tackling his art teacher.

Chapter Thirty
BUSTED

Carson sat on an uncomfortable wooden chair in Vice Principal Meehan's office.

He had managed to stop Mr. Rao from erasing himself. He had even managed to grab the eraser back and put it in his pocket after Mr. Rao dropped it. But now he was awaiting punishment from Vice Principal Meehan. And Vice Principal

Meehan was a master of punishment.

"So, Mr. Carson Cooper, I have been told that you tackled your art teacher," Vice Principal Meehan said as he glared across his desk.

Carson couldn't deny the truth. There were too many witnesses. "Yessir, I did," he said.

"Hmm," Vice Principal Meehan said. "I

appreciate your honesty. And I'm going to have to tell you that this is a first for me. I've never had a student who tackled a teacher before."

Carson hung his head. "It was a misunderstanding."

"Okay," Vice Principal Meehan said. "So help me understand the misunderstanding. Why would you do that?"

Carson wanted to tell him about Locker 37, about the magic eraser, about Hunter Barnes. About everything. But he couldn't.

"I guess . . . I didn't want to work on my self-portrait at that moment," Carson said, which was technically true. He wanted to save Mr. Rao at that moment.

"Well, I think it backfired on you, son," Vice Principal Meehan said. "Because I spoke to Mr. Rao while you were on your way down here. And together, we have decided upon a punishment that fits the crime."

"What's that?" Carson asked.

"Mr. Rao has requested that you stay after school today and create five self-portraits," he said. "Maybe in the process, you'll discover what it is that's making you so angry."

"But it's the first day," Carson said. "Plus, I've never been asked to stay after school."

"Well, you've never tackled a teacher before, have you?" Vice Principal Meehan said.

This was undeniably true.

And what else could Carson say? He couldn't admit the whole truth. And there was no way that he'd figure out how to get Hunter back now. His only comfort was knowing he'd saved Mr. Rao. That alone was worth the punishment.

"Yessir," Carson said. "I understand."

"I've already called your parents," Vice Principal Meehan told him. "They were disappointed, but they understand. First days are tough, but we cannot ignore such outbursts. Once you've finished your assignment, they will take you home."

Carson wondered what would be left of the school at that point. Certain kids always complained about how much they hated going to Hopewell Elementary. And there were thirty-one other magic erasers out there.

How long would it take until the entire building was gone?

Chapter Thirty-One

COWARDS AND HEROES

The building was still standing when Carson walked away from Vice Principal Meehan's office. Well, the hallway was still standing, at least.

Art class wasn't quite over, and there were still about twelve minutes before science class with Mrs. Shen started. Carson considered going back to Locker 37 again and begging it for another solution to his problems. But the last time they checked it, the locker was empty. He assumed it would be empty again.

So he was tempted to run, and keep running, and to never look back. Maybe he'd live in the woods for a while. Maybe in a cave. Somewhere away from all his mistakes. It was the cowardly thing to do, and Carson said to himself, "But I'm a coward, aren't I?"

"No, you're not," a voice answered. "You're very brave."

It wasn't some almighty power speaking to him. It was just a mighty power. Keisha standing behind him.

She had a bathroom pass hanging around her neck and a paper bag in her hand. She gave the paper bag to Carson.

"Is this your lunch?" Carson asked.

"That, buddy, is thirty-one erasers," Keisha said. "If you still have yours, then now you have all thirty-two."

Carson opened the bag. Sure enough, all the erasers were there.

"But . . . how?" he asked.

"Word travels fast," Keisha said. "When everyone heard how you saved Mr. Rao from erasing himself, they realized how dangerous these things could be. And they realized how big a hero you are. So it was easy to convince them to give the erasers back."

"Even you?" Carson asked.

"Not at first, but then I remembered that I don't need magic to succeed," Keisha said as she tapped her finger on her own forehead. "All my magic is up here."

Carson checked the bag again to make sure he wasn't imagining things.

He wasn't.

"Thank you," he said.

"Well, they're your problem now, Mr. Hero," Keisha said. "Personally, I was thinking of flushing them all down the toilet."

"I don't know if that's the best idea," he said, flashing back to the Dungeon toilet geyser.

No.

The best idea was to make them disappear.

So Carson tore a piece of paper from the bag. He placed the torn paper on the floor and then set all the erasers on it, except for the one he had in his pocket.

Using the eraser from his pocket, Carson started erasing erasers. He knew if he slipped, he would only erase the paper bag.

One by one, the erasers disappeared. Even though she said she was okay with it, Keisha cringed each time it happened. Carson even thought he heard her whisper, "So much lost potential."

When Carson had erased all the erasers except for the one in his hand, he said, "All done."

"What about that one?" Keisha asked. "You can't rub it on itself, can you?"

"I don't think so," Carson said. "I guess I should put it somewhere no one will find it. Somewhere it can't cause any more trouble. Problem is, I don't know where that might be."

Keisha thought about it for a moment and then said, "There's a dumpster behind the school. All the trash in it is brought to a landfill. If you put the eraser in the dumpster then the worst that can happen is it will rub up against some other trash. Then a bunch of trash will disappear. That's not so bad, is it?"

"No, that's not so bad," Carson said. "I guess it's actually kinda environmentally friendly."

"It's settled, then," Keisha said. "I've gotta get this bathroom pass back because there are, like, three minutes left in art class. Then there are five minutes after that until science class starts. Think you can get rid of that thing and get to class in eight minutes?"

The dumpster was at the far end of the school, the opposite end from Mrs. Shen's classroom. It would be tough, but . . . Carson was a hero, wasn't he?

"You better believe I can," he said.

Chapter Thirty-Two

THE "THIS CAN'T BE A CHAPTER ABOUT DUMPSTERS, CAN IT?" CHAPTER?

Do you know where the word *dumpster* comes from?

Of course you don't. You're a kid. You don't study the origins of words for large standardized metal trash containers.

The word *dumpster* actually goes back to the 1930s, when some brothers with the last name Dempster introduced large standardized metal trash containers to

the industry of waste removal. These containers could be easily loaded and unloaded onto garbage trucks, such as the Dempsters' own garbage truck, the Dempster Dumpmaster.

The Dempsters' invention became

known as a dumpster, because how could you call it anything else?

The Dempster brothers were long gone by the time Carson was in fourth grade, but there were more dumpsters in the world than ever, and that included the one behind Hopewell Elementary.

But here's the thing. No one knew who put the dumpster behind Hopewell Elementary.

It had arrived on that first morning the school became known as Hopewell Elementary. It showed up a few moments after that group of fourth-graders sang that school song and stomped that crack into the foundation.

"I guess we've got a new dumpster," the janitor said when he noticed it that evening. Then he shrugged and tossed a trash bag into it.

Every evening after that, the janitor would toss some more trash into it. And every Monday, the dumpster would be empty. That janitor retired and a new janitor joined the school, and the cycle continued like this for many years.

They'd fill the dumpster and the dumpster would be emptied. No one ever asked who emptied it. The school wasn't charged any extra money, and so what reason did they have to worry? Everything ran smoothly and the dumpster served its main purpose.

But this dumpster had more than one purpose. This dumpster was a special dumpster that did more than collect trash. This dumpster had been waiting a long time to serve its other purpose.

And what was that other purpose?

To help Carson, obviously.

Chapter Thirty-Three

UNERASABLE?

Carson bent over and took long, deep breaths. He had sprinted all the way to the dumpster in four minutes. He had four minutes to throw out the eraser and then sprint back and make it to Mrs. Shen's classroom on time.

He could do this.

But did he want to do this?

Because of a simple stain on his pants:

- Carson had temporarily flooded the school basement and gym.
- He had caused a cockroach rain.
- He had tackled an art teacher.
- And he had made a fellow student disappear.
- That's not to mention the various things his classmates had erased.

Getting rid of this last piece of eraser seemed like a good idea. But would it solve anything?

Would it bring Hunter back?

He pulled the last bit of eraser out of the pocket of the jeans he was borrowing from Bryce. He held it up to the light. And he asked himself, "What would a hero do?"

He decided that a hero would use the eraser to erase Locker 37 so that these sorts of mistakes would never happen again.

It might've seemed tough, but heroes make tough decisions. They make sacrifices. They give up their power when their power becomes too dangerous.

Carson took in a long, loud breath. But just as he was about to slip the eraser back in his pocket and run to Locker 37, Carson heard the one word that is always meant for heroes.

"Help!"

Chapter Thirty-Four

DUMPSTER DIVING

elp!"

It was a boy's voice. It was a faint voice. It was a . . . wet voice?

That was the best way Carson could describe it. It sounded wet. Or bubbly, maybe. Like someone swimming with their mouth half in the water.

"Where are you?" Carson asked.

"Over here," the voice said. "The

water . . . is so high . . . I can . . . barely . . . get my lips . . . above it."

The voice was coming from the dumpster.

Carson ran over and grabbed the dumpster's lid. He pushed it up, but it wouldn't budge. It was either stuck or locked. But he didn't see a lock anywhere.

He punched the lid, pulled it, and pushed it again, as hard as he could. It didn't move an inch.

"I can't get it open," Carson said to the dumpster.

"Please do something," the voice replied. "Whatever you can."

It didn't take Carson long to decide what to do. Someone was in trouble and his only option was to erase the dumpster.

He rubbed it one time, two times, three times, and . . .

The eraser disappeared.

"Huh," Carson said, staring at his empty hand.

But while he was staring at his hand, the dumpster disappeared, too. And everything that was inside the dumpster came pouring out on a wave of water that knocked Carson to his back.

There was:

- A brick and a doorknob
- A chair and a toilet tank
- Some heating vents and a terrarium
- An egg and a janitor closet door

- A soggy roll of toilet paper and a NO SKATEBOARDING sign
- A blade of grass and a rock
- Some trash cans and a bunch of previously frozen fish sticks
- And, finally . . . Hunter Barnes

In other words, everything that had disappeared was inside of that dumpster. It didn't seem possible, but there it all was, spread out on the wet concrete and grass behind Hopewell Elementary.

Except for the dumpster. And any sign of the eraser.

Both of those things were now gone. Both had returned to wherever they had come from. Both had served all their purposes.

Hunter stood up and shook his body to get the water off.

Carson stood up as well. He shook, too. But not to get the water off himself. He shook out of fear.

Hunter wasn't bigger or stronger than Carson. But Hunter still terrified Carson. Especially now that Hunter would be holding a grudge.

You know, for the whole erasing-his-body incident?

The two boys stared at each other for a few seconds, but didn't say anything. The silence was painfully awkward. So Carson finally spoke.

"You missed some classes," he said.

"Wouldn't be the first time," Hunter replied.

"If we run right now, we'll make it to science before it starts," Carson said.

"I guess that's what we should do, then," Hunter said.

"So? Should we . . . ?" Carson asked.

But neither boy moved.

They stared at each other for another awkward moment.

And then Hunter said, "You don't still have that eraser, do you?"

Carson thought about what to say. It's worth repeating that Carson wasn't a liar. But it's also worth repeating that Carson didn't always reveal the whole truth.

"Just a minute ago, that eraser was in the pocket of these jeans," Carson said.

"Those jeans?" Hunter asked, pointing.

"Yep," Carson said. "These jeans."

Hunter took a step back. Then he smiled, but not in a happy way. In a nervous way. And he said, "They're very . . . nice jeans."

Chapter Thirty-Five

MRS. SHEN AGAIN

Mrs. Shen stood at the whiteboard as Carson and Hunter busted through the door and into her classroom. She looked at her watch.

"Ten seconds to spare," she said. "Have a seat, gentlemen."

Carson chose to sit near the windows, next to Riley. Hunter chose to sit as far away from Carson as possible.

"Holy linguine fra diavolo," Riley whispered. "You did it. But how?"

"The eraser," Carson said.

"I was right," Riley said. "As always."

From across the room, Bryce waved at Carson and then gave him a thumbs-up.

And Keisha walked up to Carson on her way to her seat in the back next to the goldfish bowl. She patted him on the shoulder as she passed.

All the attention didn't necessarily make Carson feel good. But it didn't make him feel nervous, either. He felt relieved for the first time all day.

"Carson?" Mrs. Shen said. "I trust we won't be having any more incidents like the one I heard about in your art class?"

"No, ma'am," Carson said.

"Good," Mrs. Shen said. "Because I didn't wear my football pads today."

The class laughed.

"And Hunter?" Mrs. Shen said. "I believe you missed some classes today. Care to offer an explanation?"

A worried look fell over Hunter's face. "I sorta disappeared for a while."

"Disappeared?" Mrs. Shen said.

Hunter nodded.

"Well, everyone will be happy that you reappeared," Mrs. Shen said. "Your parents especially."

Hunter stood up.

"Where are you going?" Mrs. Shen asked.

"To Vice Principal Meehan's office," Hunter said with a sigh. "Like always."

Mrs. Shen shook her head and told him, "Sit. There will be no punishment for you today."

There was a gleam in Mrs. Shen's eye, the type of look someone has when they're in on a joke.

Could she possibly know about Locker 37?

Carson couldn't tell. And he certainly couldn't ask.

"Why am I not being punished?" Hunter asked as he sat down.

Mrs. Shen smiled and replied, "I'm making an exception because somehow you've managed to break the laws of thermodynamics."

"I didn't break any laws," Hunter said. "It's not illegal to miss a few classes."

Mrs. Shen chuckled. "I'm not talking about our legal system. I'm talking about the laws of the universe. Which is actually a good way to introduce today's subject. Who here has heard of the big bang?"

Keisha raised her hand and when she was called on, she said, "It's how the universe started. The universe was once teeny-tiny, like smaller than a pinprick, but then all of a sudden it got really big."

"That's more or less correct," Mrs. Shen said. "And this all happened about 13.7 billion years ago."

"That's . . . a long time ago," Bryce said.

"It is indeed," Mrs. Shen said. "But all the stuff that was in the universe back then is still here. The black holes.

The stars. The planets. This school. Your bodies. It all comes from the big bang. The stuff that makes up the universe has always been here. It might rearrange itself into new configurations, but it never truly disappears. So that's why I said Hunter broke the laws of thermodynamics when he said he disappeared."

"Okay," Hunter replied. "I guess I didn't really disappear, then. I guess I sorta rearranged myself into a new configuration."

"And what configuration is that?" Riley asked.

There was a strange look on Hunter's face. Was he mad? Was he scared? Was he confused?

It was hard to read. And Hunter's words didn't make things any clearer.

"I'm not sure yet," Hunter said as he turned and looked at Carson.

But, for the moment, that was good enough for Carson.

Chapter Thirty-Six
SOLUTIONS

The bell announcing the end of the school day rang. By now, all the fourth-graders knew about Locker 37. And they were all pitching in to return the previously erased objects to their original locations.

Except for the fish sticks. Not even Riley wanted those soggy messes.

Carson was on his way to the art room,

where he was going to create five self-portraits. He thought he might use paint, clay, pastels, pens, and pencils to make the five versions. But even if he made some mistakes, he was not going to be using any erasers.

During his walk to the art room, Carson passed the main stairway to the basement. He heard some voices coming from the Dungeon.

He had a few extra minutes to spare, so he went down to investigate.

Bryce, Keisha, and Riley were inside the Dungeon, trying to reattach the toilet tank to the broken toilet.

"Well, if any of us are plumbers, then we need to go back to plumbing school. How 'bout we leave the tank on the floor and be done with it?" Riley said.

"Fine with me," Keisha said, putting her hands up and backing away. "No one ever uses this thing, anyway."

"Maybe we *should* use it," Bryce said. "Not the toilet, but the room. Maybe this could be, like, our meeting place to talk about Locker 37."

It wasn't a bad idea. The hallway that led to Locker 37 was private, but the Dungeon was absolutely desolate. For good reason, too. It was not a pleasant place.

"We should probably redecorate first, though," Riley said.

Carson was indebted to his friends for seeing him through the most difficult and exciting day of his life. Each one of them had helped him out immensely.

So he made his presence known by saying, "Thank you."

"Oh, hey, Carson," Bryce replied. "What are you thanking us for?"

"For . . . everything," Carson said. "Starting with these jeans. I'll wash them tonight and get them back to you tomorrow."

"Or you could just give them to him now," Riley said. "Look what I found."

Riley held up Carson's pants. The pants he had put on that morning, the ones with the stain. Only they didn't have a stain on them anymore.

Carson hurried over and grabbed them.

"Where did you find them?" he asked.

"They were hanging over one of the stall doors," Riley said.

Carson gave the pants a close look.

"Where did the stain go?" he asked. "I never erased it."

"Maybe all that water washed it off," Bryce said.

It was certainly possible.

Carson reached into the pocket of the pants. The note was still there. He took it out and read it again. This time, one sentence in particular stuck with him.

It won't always be the solution you want, or expect, but it is guaranteed to work.

No, this wasn't the solution Carson had wanted.

It definitely wasn't the one he'd expected.

But yes, it had worked.

Chapter Thirty-Seven

COMING NEXT . . .

When Keisha James forgets to do her science homework, she thinks her lifetime of good grades is over. But the magical Locker 37 gifts her with a clock that can literally rewind time, and Keisha knows she can't waste her second (or third . . . or fourth) chance. Keisha only has so much time to make things right— so how will she use it?